Phonics Friends

Umeko and
the Music Show
The Sound of Long U

The
**Child's
World**

By Cecilia Minden and Joanne Meier

Published in the United States of America
by The Child's World®
PO Box 326
Chanhassen, MN 55317-0326
800-599-READ
www.childsworld.com

The Child's World®: Mary Berendes, Publishing Director

A special thank you to Mary Ravid, principal of O. A.
Thorp Scholastic Academy, Debra Grimes and her
music students, and the Shirihama family and its star
performer Taylor.

Editorial Directions, Inc.: E. Russell Primm, Editorial
Director and Project Editor; Katie Marsico, Associate
Editor; Judith Shiffer, Associate Editor and School Media
Specialist; Linda S. Koutris, Photo Researcher and
Selector

The Design Lab: Kathleen Petelinsek, Design and Page
Production

Photographs ©: Photo setting and photography by Romie
and Alice Flanagan/Flanagan Publishing Services: cover,
4, 6, 8, 10, 14, 16, 18, 20; Getty Images/Taxi/Michael
Krasowitz: 12.

Library of Congress Cataloging-in-Publication Data
Minden, Cecilia.
  Umeko and the music show : the sound of long U /
by Cecilia Minden and Joanne Meier.
     p. cm. — (Phonics friends)
  Summary: Umeko appears in a music show and sings
with her friends, in simple text featuring the long "u"
sound.
  ISBN 1-59296-321-8 (library bound : alk. paper)
  [1. English language—Phonetics. 2. Reading.] I. Meier,
Joanne D. II. Title. III. Series.
  PZ7.M6539Um 2004
  [E]—dc22
                                                    2004002235

Note to parents and educators:

*The Child's World® has created Phonics Friends with
the goal of exposing children to engaging stories and
pictures that assist in phonics development. The books
in the series will help children learn the relationships
between the letters of written language and the indi-
vidual sounds of spoken language. This contact helps
children learn to use these relationships to read and
write words.*

*The books in this series follow a similar format.
An introductory page, to be read by an adult, intro-
duces the child to the phonics feature, or sound, that
will be highlighted in the book. Read this page to the
child, stressing the phonic feature. Help the student
learn how to form the sound with her mouth. The
Phonics Friends story and engaging photographs follow
the introduction. At the end of the story, word lists
categorize the feature words into their phonic element.
Additional information on using these lists is on The
Child's World® Web site listed at the top of this page.*

*Each book in this series has been carefully written
to meet specific readability requirements. Close atten-
tion has been paid to elements such as word count,
sentence length, and vocabulary. Readability formulas
measure the ease with which the text can be read and
understood. Each Phonics Friends book has been ana-
lyzed using the Spache readability formula. For more
information on this formula, as well as the levels for
each of the books in this series please visit The Child's
World® Web site.*

*Reading research suggests that systematic phonics
instruction can greatly improve students' word recogni-
tion, spelling, and comprehension skills. The Phonics
Friends series assists in the teaching of phonics by
providing students with important opportunities to
apply their knowledge of phonics as they read words,
sentences, and text.*

The letter *u* makes two sounds.

The short sound of *u* sounds like *u* as in:

 mud and *up*.

The long sound of *u* sounds like *u* as in:

 cute and *tube*.

In this book, you will read words that have the long *u* sound as in:

 music, blue, fruit, and *juice*.

Umeko is in a show.

Her class practices many tunes.

The music is so pretty!

Umeko wears a blue dress.

She takes her usual place

in line.

The children sing loudly.

They use their best voices.

Their parents clap hands.

"You are great!" they call.

Umeko is happy and proud.

We did it!

After the show the children

have a party. There are blue

flowers on the table.

The parents and children eat cake. They drink fruit juice. What a treat!

Umeko has a huge smile

on her face.

Fun Facts

You probably own a pair of blue jeans, but you might not know that these pants aren't completely blue! Blue jeans typically contain both blue and white threads. Can people be blue, too? If someone says you seem blue, that person is telling you that you look sad. Is your blood blue? No, all human beings have red blood, but someone who comes from a royal family might be described as "blue-blooded."

Are you able to play a musical instrument such as the piano or violin? Wolfgang Amadeus Mozart is one of the world's most famous musicians and lived in the 1700s. Even as a young boy, Mozart enjoyed music. He was playing music when he was four years old and was writing his own music when he was five. Another well-known musician, Ludwig van Beethoven, lived in the late 1700s and early 1800s. Even though Beethoven became deaf, he continued to compose beautiful music.

Activity

Making a Blue Noodle Necklace
Would you like to own a piece of blue jewelry to match your blue jeans? Gather some dry pasta noodles—tube-shaped noodles such as mostaccioli or rigatoni would work best. Paint the noodles blue and let them dry for a few hours. Next, string the noodles along a piece of blue yarn. Tie the ends of the yarn in a knot, and simply place your new necklace over your head!

To Learn More

Books
About the Sound of Long U
Noyed, Robert B., and Cynthia Klingel. *Cute! The Sound of Long U.* Chanhassen, Minn.: The Child's World, 2000.

About Blue
Boynton, Sandra. *Blue Hat, Green Hat.* New York: Little Simon, 1984.

Johnson, Stephen T. *My Little Blue Robot.* San Diego: Silver Whistle/Harcourt, 2002.

Rodrigue, George, and Bruce Goldstone. *Why Is Blue Dog Blue?: A Tale of Colors.* New York: Stewart, Tabori & Chang, 2001.

About Music
Krull, Kathleen, and Stacy Innerst (illustrator). *M is for Music.* Orlando: Harcourt, 2003.

Lithgow, John, and C. F. Payne (illustrator). *The Remarkable Farkle McBride.* New York: Simon & Schuster for Young Readers, 2000.

Martin, Bill Jr., and Sal Murdocca (illustrator). *Maestro Plays.* New York: Holt, Rinehart, and Winston, 1970.

Web Sites
Visit our home page for lots of links about the Sound of Long U:

http://www.childsworld.com/links.html

Note to Parents, Teachers, and Librarians: We routinely check our Web links to make sure they're safe, active sites—so encourage your readers to check them out!

Long U
Feature Words

Proper Names

Umeko

**Feature Words with
Consonant–Vowel–Silent E
Pattern**

huge

tune

use

**Feature Words with
Other Vowel Patterns**

blue

fruit

juice

music

usual

you

About the Authors

*Cecilia Minden, PhD,
directs the Language and
Literacy Program at the
Harvard Graduate School
of Education. She is a
reading specialist with
classroom and administrative experience in
grades K–12. She earned her PhD in reading
education from the University of Virginia.
Cecilia and her husband Dave Cupp enjoy
sharing their love of reading with their
granddaughter Chelsea.*

*Joanne Meier, PhD, has
worked as an elementary
school teacher and
university professor. She
earned her BA in early
childhood education from
the University of South Carolina, and her MEd
and PhD in education from the University
of Virginia. She currently works as a literacy
consultant for schools and private organizations.
Joanne Meier lives with her husband Eric,
and spends most of her time chasing her two
daughters, Kella and Erin, and her two cats,
Sam and Gilly, in Charlottesville, Virginia.*